# MY VERY OWN YOM KIPPUR BOOK
## by
### Judyth Robbins Saypol
### Madeline Wikler

. . . *upon Israel*
*and upon their children and upon all the children of their*
*children*
*in this place and in every place,*
*to them and to you*
*life.*

—Charles Reznikoff
"Kaddish"
*By the Waters of Manhattan*

ISBN 0-930494-05-9
Published by KAR-BEN Copies, 11713 Auth Lane, Silver Spring, MD 20902 (301) 593-2563.
Printed in the United States of America.

Rosh Hashanah and Yom Kippur are not children's holidays. The ideas they express are difficult even for adults. Yet children are aware that these are the central religious holidays of the Jewish year. They stay home from school. They participate in family celebrations and the sending and receiving of *Shanah Tovah* cards. They attend children's synagogue services.

Our books — one for each of the holidays — should be seen as resources to help young children understand such Rosh Hashanah and Yom Kippur ideas as renewal, forgiveness, repentence, responsibility. Both the narrative and the *Chassidic* stories which illustrate many of the High Holy Day themes, can be used as starting points for family or classroom discussion.

J.R.S.
M.W.

osh Hashanah and Yom Kippur are a new beginning.

Why do we need a new beginning?

Because —

We do things we wish we had not done.

We make promises we wish we had not made.

We say things we wish we had not said.

We need a chance to start all over again.

Beginning on Rosh Hashanah, and for the next ten days, we think about the year that has passed and the year that is to come. On the tenth day we celebrate Yom Kippur, the Day of Forgiveness. It is the holiest day of the Jewish year.

Yom Kippur gives us a chance —

To ask our friends and family to forgive us.

To forgive those with whom we have been angry.

To try to make the new year better than the last one.

# ON YOM KIPPUR GOD FORGIVES US

Have you ever made a promise to God? Many people, children and grown-ups alike, make promises when they pray to God.

Promises like —

*Dear God, Please help me pass my spelling test, and I will always do my homework.*

*Dear God, please help grandma get well, and I will always be nice to her.*

*Dear God, please let me have a new bicycle for my birthday, and I will always share it with my brother.*

If we can't keep these promises, we feel bad.

Sometimes we are afraid we will be punished.

Jewish people believe that God is forgiving. God does not expect us to be perfect. He forgives us —

When we say we are sorry.

When we try to do better.

When we are helpful to others.

# ON YOM KIPPUR WE FORGIVE EACH OTHER

But God can forgive us only for promises we make to Him. We also make promises to our friends and family.

We promise our parents we will be helpful.

We promise our friends we will play fairly.

We promise our sisters and brothers we will share.

We promise our teachers we will try harder.

Sometimes we don't keep these promises, either.

On Yom Kippur we have the chance to ask our friends and family for forgiveness, too.

It is hard to ask for forgiveness. It is hard to say, "I'm sorry." But it is important to say it, and to mean it.

It tells people that we care about them.

It is even harder to forgive others when they hurt us. On Yom Kippur, just as we ask others to forgive us, we try to forgive them. When someone says to us, "I'm sorry," we should say, "That's okay. Let's be friends again."

There was once a poor countrywoman who had many children. They were always begging for food, but she had none to give them.

One day she found an egg. She called her children and said, "Children, children, we have nothing to worry about anymore; I have found an egg.

"And being a wise woman, I shall not let us eat the egg, but I shall ask my neighbor permission to put it under her hen until it hatches into a baby chick.

"And we shall not eat the baby chick, but shall let it grow until it lays more eggs which will hatch into more chicks.

"But we will not eat even these. Since I am such

a wise woman, I shall sell them and use the money to buy a cow.

"But we shall not eat the cow. Instead, we will let it grow, and the cow will have baby calves.

"And since I am such a wise woman, I shall sell them and use the money to buy a field.

"And we will have fields, and cows, and calves, and chickens, and eggs.

"And we will not be hungry anymore."

While the countrywoman spoke, she turned the egg round and round in her hands. Suddenly it slipped, fell to the ground, and broke.

We are all like the countrywoman. We make many vows and promises. We say to ourselves, "I promise to do this, and I promise to do that." But the days slip by, and our prom- ises do not lead to action.

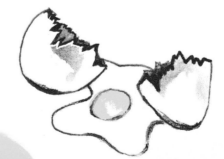

# YOM KIPPUR IS A FAST DAY

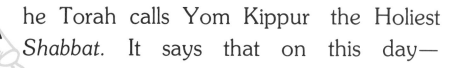

he Torah calls Yom Kippur the Holiest *Shabbat.* It says that on this day—

We should not work.

We should ask forgiveness for our sins.

We should punish ourselves.

This punishment has come to mean that we fast — we do not eat or drink.

We fast on Yom Kippur for other reasons as well —

To have more time to think and pray.

To know how poor people feel when they are hungry.

Jewish law says that children should not fast until after their *Bar* or *Bat Mitzvah.* But younger children should be taught how to fast. When you are five or six, you can begin by skipping snacks. When you are nine or ten, you can skip a meal — breakfast or lunch. Over the years, you can build up the strength to fast for the whole day.

# YOM KIPPUR AT HOME

Yom Kippur begins in the evening with the *Kol Nidre* service. We eat an early dinner in order to arrive at the synagogue on time. This final meal before our fast is festive. Even though Yom Kippur is a serious holiday, it is not a sad one. We are hopeful that we will be forgiven for our sins, and that the new year will be one of happiness, health, and peace.

We do not say *Kiddush* over wine because our meal is eaten before Yom Kippur begins. We share round *challah* as we did on Rosh Hashanah.

Before leaving for synagogue, it is a custom in some homes to cover the dinner table with a white cloth and put Jewish books on it. This is a way of saying that we celebrate Yom Kippur by fasting, prayer, and serious thought.

In addition to lighting the usual holiday candles, some families light *yahrzeit* or memorial candles to remember relatives who have died. These candles will burn through the night and all the next day.

# KOL NIDRE

**M**any people think *Kol Nidre* is the most beautiful synagogue service of the year. It takes its name from the *Kol Nidre* prayer, in which we ask God's forgiveness for all the promises we make to Him and do not keep. It is sung to the same melody in nearly every synagogue in the world.

On Yom Kippur, the Rabbi and Cantor dress in white robes called *kittels.* Even the *Torah* scrolls are dressed in white. White stands for forgiveness. In the synagogues where the *tallit* or prayer shawl is used, this is the only time when it is worn at an evening service.

At the beginning of the service, leaders of the congregation open the Ark, take out all of the *Torah* scrolls, and stand beside the Cantor while he chants the *Kol Nidre.* The prayer is sung three times, each time a little louder. Often a choir or the congregation join in.

One Yom Kippur a Rabbi imagined he stood before God and had the following conversation:
God asked him:

"Have you studied all you should?"

The Rabbi said,

"No."

Then he was asked:

"Have you prayed all you should?"

Again he answered,

"No."

He was asked a third question:

"Have you done all the good you should?"

And this time, too, he said,

"No."

And God proclaimed:

"You have told the truth, and for the sake of truth, you will be forgiven."

# YOM KIPPUR DAY

Yom Kippur prayers are very long. There are readings from the Torah, and a memorial service. Many grown-ups stay in the synagogue all day. Most synagogues have special services and activities for children.

In the prayers on Yom Kippur we confess our sins and pray for forgiveness. To confess means to tell the truth about something you did wrong.

If your mother asks you, "Did you break the glass?" and you answer, "Yes, I did," you are confessing.

Jewish people believe that we should ask forgiveness, not only for our own sins, but for the sins of others as well. When we confess, we say, "We have sinned," and not, "I have sinned."

Sometimes we sin because of what we have done, and sometimes we sin because of what we have not done. The Confession we read on Yom Kippur talks about both kinds of sins.

For the sins we have sinned before You:

Gossiping and telling lies
Causing someone else to sin
Being rude to parents and teachers
Being unfriendly or hateful
Wanting what someone else has
Taking something that doesn't belong to us

Not admitting our mistakes
Not being fair
Not stopping someone else from sinning
Not helping someone in trouble
Not keeping promises

For all of these sins, God of forgiveness,
forgive us and pardon us this Yom Kippur.

13

Once there was a child who loved to tell stories about his friends. Sometimes the stories were true, and sometimes the stories were not quite true. The neighborhood children did not like their gossiping friend. One day they decided to ask the Rabbi's advice.

The Rabbi heard their complaints, and called the child to his house.

"Why do you make up stories about your friends?" the Rabbi asked.

"It's only talk," replied the child. "I can always take it back."

"Perhaps you are right," said the Rabbi, and he began to talk of other things.

As the child was ready to leave, the Rabbi asked, "I wonder if you would do something for me."

"Of course," said the child.

The Rabbi took a pillow from the couch and handed it to the child. "Take this pillow to the town square. When you get there, cut it open, and shake out the feathers. Then come back."

The child was puzzled, but agreed to do what the Rabbi said. He carried the pillow to the town square and cut it open. The breeze scattered the feathers across the sky.

The child returned to the Rabbi's house and told him what he had done.

The Rabbi seemed pleased. He handed the boy a basket and said, "Now please go back to the square, and gather the feathers up again."

The child gasped. "But that's impossible."

"You are right," said the Rabbi. "So it is not possible to take back all the untrue things you said about others. Be careful with the words you spread. Once spoken and sent on their way, they cannot be gathered again."

# MEMORIAL PRAYERS

An important part of Yom Kippur is the *Yizkor,* or memorial service. If someone in your family has died, your parents probably attend this service.

Even though it is sad to think about those who have died, Jewish people believe that it is important to remember them.

We remember —

the happy times we shared with them,
their good deeds, and
the things they taught us.

We also honor their memory by promising on Yom Kippur to give *tzedakah* to synagogues, schools, and organizations in the community.

# NEILAH

All during Yom Kippur we pray that the gates of heaven will be opened to let in our prayers. The final service is called *Neilah*, which means closing — the closing of the day and the closing of the gates of prayer.

We end Yom Kippur with the *Sh'ma* —

שְׁמַע יִשְׂרָאֵל יְיָ אֱלֹהֵינוּ יְיָ אֶחָד :

*Sh'ma Yisrael Adonai Eloheinu Adonai Echad.*

Here O Israel, the Lord Our God the Lord is One.

Then comes one long blast of the *Shofar*.

We wish each other a good new year and hurry home to end our fast. After eating, some families begin preparations for the next holiday, *Sukkot*, which comes five days later. Sometimes they even hammer the first nail into their *Sukkah*.

Long ago in a small village there lived a young boy. He was a shepherd and had never gone to school. He spent his days watching his sheep and playing his flute, which he loved very much.

One year be begged his father to go to the synagogue on Yom Kippur. He took his flute along.

The shepherd boy listened to the beautiful praying and singing. He wanted to join in, but did not know how to pray.

Then he remembered his flute and asked to play it for God. His father warned the boy not to disturb the congregation.

During the afternoon service the boy asked again, and again his father said, "No."

Finally the time came for Neilah, *the closing prayer. Suddenly the boy could not hold back any longer. He took the flute from his pocket,* put it to his lips, and played. He played the sound that he felt in his heart.

His father became angry.

But the Rabbi turned to him and

said, "All Yom Kippur I have prayed hard so that our sins might be forgiven. But I felt that my prayers were not heard. When this little boy played on his flute, I knew at once the gates of heaven had opened. The boy's simple song to God came from his heart, and through him, all our prayers were lifted to heaven."

20

# HOME SERVICE FOR EREV YOM KIPPUR

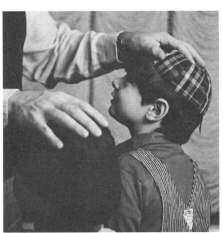

# TZEDAKAH

In many synagogues on the afternoon before Yom Kippur, plates are set out on a large table. Each plate has the name of a Jewish school, hospital, or other organization. Those who come to services put money in the plates.

Giving *tzedakah*, sharing what we have, is one way of asking forgiveness on Yom Kippur.

At home, before we share our meal on Erev Yom Kippur, we set aside some of our allowance or savings for *tzedakah*.

# HAMOTZI
# BLESSING OVER THE CHALLAH

The meal before Yom Kippur is especially festive because it is the final meal before we begin our fast. As we share the *challah*, we are grateful for the blessings of life, health, love and friendship.

בָּרוּךְ אַתָּה יְיָ אֱלֹהֵינוּ מֶלֶךְ הָעוֹלָם · הַמּוֹצִיא לֶחֶם מִן הָאָרֶץ:

*Baruch atah adonai eloheinu melech*
*ha'olam hamotzi lechem min ha'aretz.*

Thank you, God, for the blessing of bread, and for the festive meal which we will now enjoy together.

# BIRKAT HAMAZON
# BLESSING AFTER THE MEAL

We join in giving thanks for the festive meal we have eaten.

בָּרוּךְ אַתָּה יְיָ · הַזָּן אֶת־הַכֹּל :

*Baruch atah adonai hazan et hakol.*

עֹשֶׂה שָׁלוֹם בִּמְרוֹמָיו הוּא יַעֲשֶׂה שָׁלוֹם
עָלֵינוּ וְעַל־כָּל־יִשְׂרָאֵל · וְאִמְרוּ אָמֵן :

*Oseh shalom bimromav hu ya'aseh shalom
aleinu ve'al kol Yisrael ve'imru amen.*

Thank you, God,
for the festive meal we have shared,
for the food we have eaten at this table,
for the Torah and *mitzvot* which guide our lives,
for Israel, the homeland of the Jewish people,
for our freedom to live as Jews,
for life, strength, and health.
Bless our family, and grant us a good year.

*(music pages 27-28)*

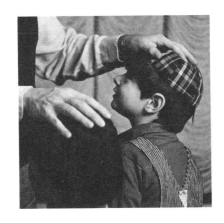

# BIRKAT HABANIM
# BLESSING THE CHILDREN

On Yom Kippur parents set aside time to bless their children. You may wish to use your own words or the traditional priestly blessing.

יְבָרֶכְךָ יְיָ וְיִשְׁמְרֶךָ :

יָאֵר יְיָ פָּנָיו אֵלֶיךָ וִיחֻנֶּךָּ :

יִשָּׂא יְיָ פָּנָיו אֵלֶיךָ וְיָשֵׂם לְךָ שָׁלוֹם :

*Y'varech'cha adonai v'yishm'recha*
*Ya'er adonai panav elecha vichuneka*
*Yisa adonai panav elecha v'yasem l'cha shalom.*

May God bless and keep you.
May He watch over you in kindness.
May He grant you a long life of good health, joy, and peace.

## HADLAKAT NEROT
## CANDLE-LIGHTING

Before leaving for the synagogue, we welcome the festival of Yom Kippur with the lighting of the candles.

בָּרוּךְ אַתָּה יְיָ אֱלֹהֵינוּ מֶלֶךְ הָעוֹלָם · אֲשֶׁר קִדְּשָׁנוּ בְּמִצְוֹתָיו וְצִוָּנוּ לְהַדְלִיק נֵר שֶׁל יוֹם הַכִּפֻּרִים

*Baruch atah adonai eloheinu melech
ha'olam asher kid'shanu b'mitzvotav
v'tzivanu l'hadlik ner shel Yom Hakippurim.*

בָּרוּךְ אַתָּה יְיָ אֱלֹהֵינוּ מֶלֶךְ הָעוֹלָם · שֶׁהֶחֱיָנוּ וְקִיְּמָנוּ וְהִגִּיעָנוּ לַזְּמַן הַזֶּה :

*Baruch atah adonai eloheinu melech
ha'olam shehecheyanu, vekiy'manu,
v'higiyanu laz'man hazeh.*

Thank you, God, for bringing our family together to celebrate Yom Kippur, and for the *mitzvah* of lighting the candles. May you forgive us and help us to forgive others. May we be blessed with a year of peace.

# BIRKAT HAMAZON

M. NATHANSON

Flowing, in a thankful manner

Ba - ruch a - tah __ a - do - nai e - lo -
hei - nu me-lech ha-o-lam ha-zan et ha-o-lam ku-lo b'-tu-vo b'-
chen b'-che-sed uv' ra-cha-mim hu no-ten le-chem l'chol ba-sar
ki l'-o-lam chas - do uv'-tu-vo ha-ga-dol ta-
mid lo cha-sar la-nu v'-al yech-sar la-nu ma - zon l'-o-lam va-ed ba-a-
vur sh'mo ha-ga-dol ____ ki hu el zan um'-far-nes la - kol u-mei-
tiv la - kol u-mei-chin ma-zon l' - chol b'ri-o-tav a - sher__ ba - ra. Baruch a - tah__ a-do - nai ____ ha-zan __ et ha - kol.

27

# OSEH SHALOM

By N. HIRSH

# LIGHTING THE CANDLES

*Freely adapted after a version by A.W. BINDER*

Freely, as a chant

Ba - ruch a - tah a - do nai e - lo - hei - nu me - lech ha -
o - lam, a - sher kid - sha - nu b'mitz - vo - tav v - tzi - va - nu l' - had - lik
ner, l' had - lik ner, shel Yom Ha - kip - pur - im.

## SHEHECHEYANU

**Traditional**

Ba - ruch a - tah a - do - nai e - lo - hei - nu me - lech ha - o - lam she -

he - che - ya - nu v' - kiy' - ma - nu v' - hi - gi - ya - nu la - z'man ha - zeh.

## L'SHANAH TOVAH

**Traditional**

L' - sha - nah to - vah ti - ka - te - vu, l' - sha - nah to - vah ti - ka -

te - vu, ti - ka - te - vu v' - te - cha - te - mu.

29

# KOL NIDRE

Traditional

Kol nid - re — v' - e - sa - re — v' - cha - ra - me — v' - ko - na -

me — v' - chi - nu - ye — v' - ki - nu - se — u - sh' - vu - ot.

# LET'S BE FRIENDS

G. GEWIRTZ

Let's be friends, make a - mends, now's the time to say I'm sor - ry.

Let's be friends, make a - mends, please say you'll for - give me. The — give me.

ten days of te - shu - vah, time to make up time to pray. —

Shake my hand, I'll — shake yours. Let's be friends for al - ways.

30

# AVINU MALKENU

Traditional

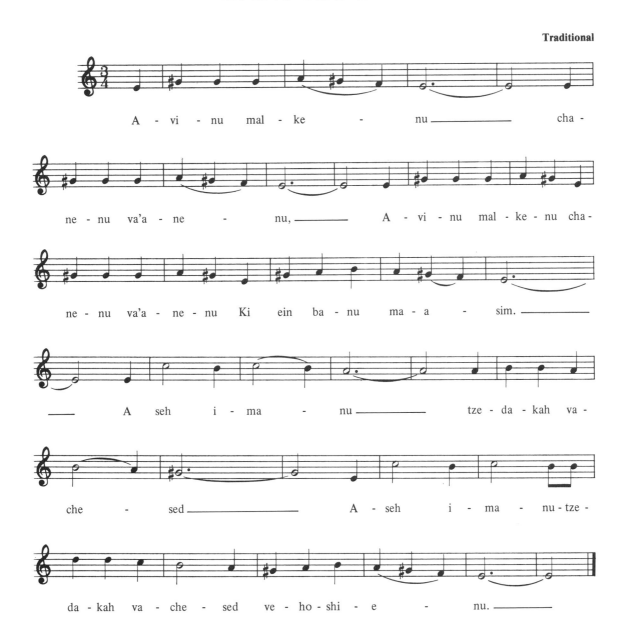

A - vi - nu mal - ke - nu _____ cha -

ne - nu va'a - ne - nu, _____ A - vi - nu mal - ke - nu cha -

ne - nu va'a - ne - nu Ki ein ba - nu ma - a - sim. _____

_____ A seh i - ma - nu _____ tze - da - kah va -

che - sed _____ A - seh i - ma - nu - tze -

da - kah va - che - sed ve - ho - shi - e - nu. _____

**31**

**OTHER KAR-BEN COPIES PUBLICATIONS**

by Judyth R. Saypol and Madeline Wikler
  *My Very Own Haggadah*
  *My Very Own Megillah*
  *My Very Own Chanukah Book*
  *My Very Own Jewish Calendar*
  *My Very Own Rosh Hashanah Book*
  *Come, Let Us Welcome Shabbat*
by Ruth Esrig Brinn
  *Let's Celebrate — 57 Jewish Holiday Crafts*